Davy's Ride Down

By Michele Gibeau Cronin

Illustrated by Ben F. Taylor

To the children of Moody School, Enjoy the ride!! ☺

Love,

Miss Michele

Davy's Ride Down

Published by Pear Tree Publishing
www.PearTreePublishing.net

First Edition

Printed in the United States of America
By Signature Book Printing, Inc. Gaithersburg, MD

Cronin, Michele Gibeau
Davy's Ride Down / by Michele Gibeau Cronin – 1st Ed.
ISBN 978-1-62502-026-0
Library of Congress Control Number: 2017958311

1. Children's Book–Author. 2. Music–Juvenile Fiction 3. Winter Sports–Juvenile Fiction 4. Imagination–Juvenile Fiction 5. Discipline-Juvenile Fiction
I. Cronin, Michele Gibeau II. Title III. Children's–Fiction

Illustrated by Ben F. Taylor
Musical Drawings by Anna M. Cronin

Cover & Book Design by Ben F. Taylor and Michele Gibeau Cronin
Author photo by Matt Cronin

Contact author at: *DavysRideDown@gmail.com*

Pear
Tree
Publishing

*For Matthew, James, Paul,
Sarah and Anna*

♡

"My name is Davy and I'm going outside.

I'm going outside and I'm going outside!"

Snow, snow, lots of snow.

Davy loves riding down the big hill.

Davy wants to play outside,

But Momma says . . .

"Practice comes first."

Davy gets his violin
and puts it under his chin.

He pulls the bow over the strings;
he likes that sound.

He moves his fingers fast.
He plays Bach; it is hard.

"My name is Davy and I wanna go outside!"

Davy is glad to put his violin away.

NOW he can go outside.

"My name is Davy and I'm going outside!
I'm going outside and I'm going outside!"

Time to get ready . . .

Snow pants on.

Pull, pull,

PULL

the boots.

Zip,

Zup,

ZWIP

the jacket.

Hat, scarf and mittens, too.
"Thank you, Momma!"

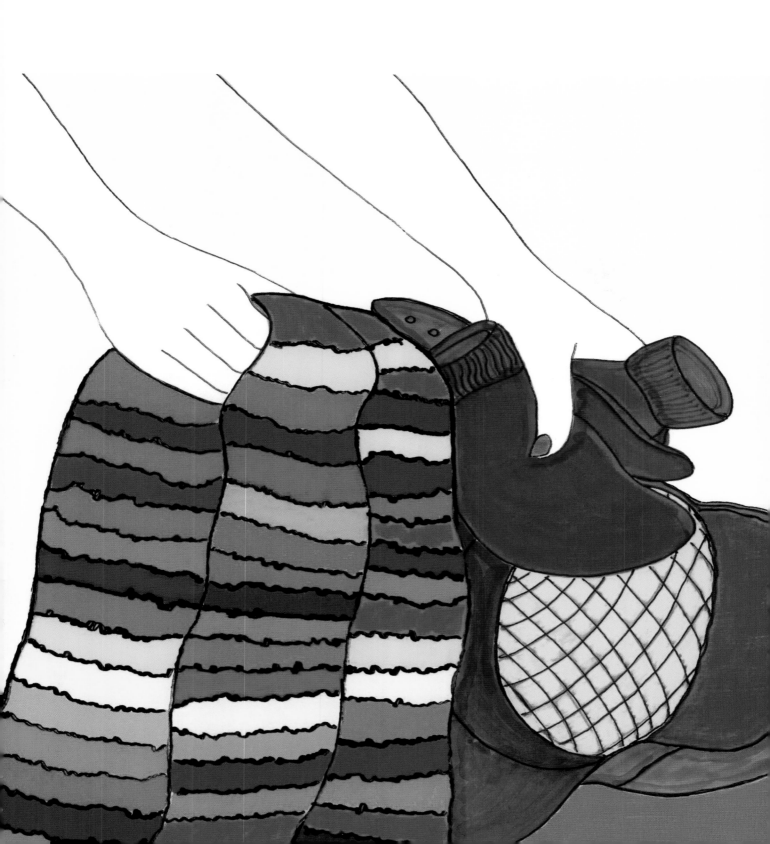

Davy is happy.

He sings a little tune as he stomps

and clomps his way to the big hill.

"My name is Davy and I'm walking around,

I'm going way up and I'm flying way down.

My name is Davy and I'm picking my nose.

I'm picking my nose and my boogers are froze."

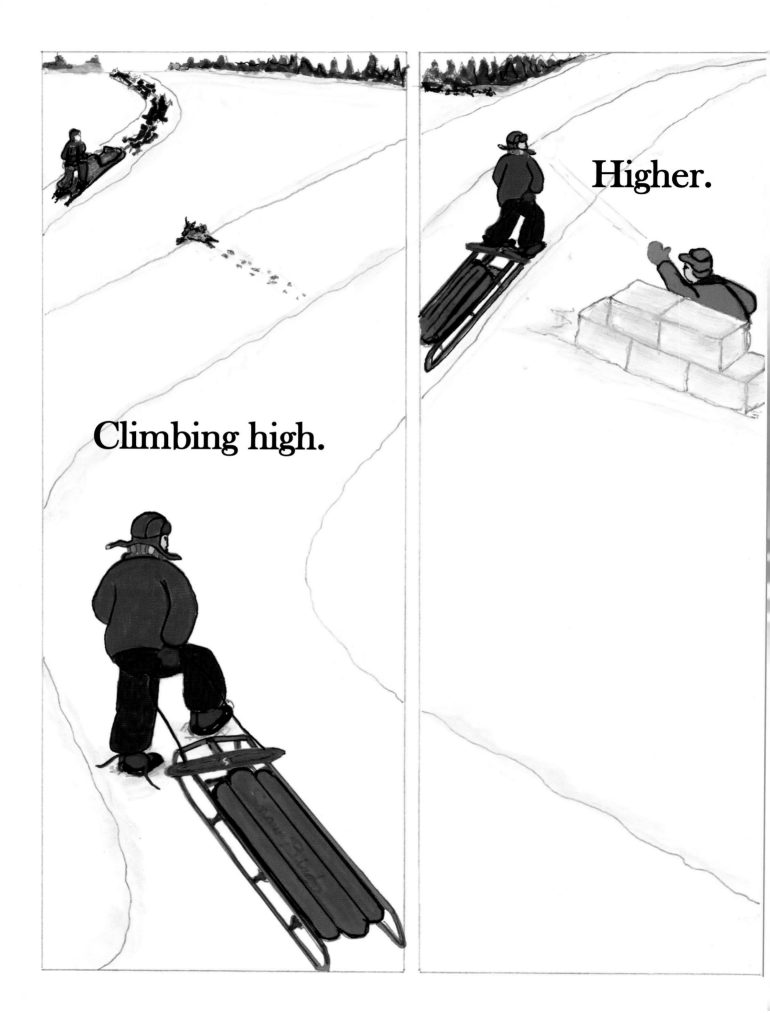

Climbing high.

Higher.

Highest.

Time to ride down . . .

"Dad, Dad–WATCH THIS!"

Going fast.

Faster.

Fastest!

So fast,

Davy's hat

flies off,

and then his scarf

spins away.

Davy flies SO fast,

his jacket . . .

ZA-ZOOOMPS!

His boots

GA-LOOOSH!

And his snow pants . . .

WOO-WOOOSH!

"StuPENdous!" shouts Dad.

Davy lands with a

FLUMPITY

BUMP!

And he says . . .

"AGAIN!"

"My name is Davy and my bum is numb.

My bum is numb and my numb is bum."

Acknowledgements

Endless gratitude flows from my heart to my illustrator friend, Ben F. Taylor. Your great ideas and clever pictures, bringing my little story to life, makes me so happy.

My lovely daughter Anna, bunches of thanks for your whimsically-designed musical staves; I love them.

You = stupendous, me = grateful to Mike, supportive husband and advocate, enduring my perpetual craziness throughout the process. For your expertise and our many hours with image processing, BIG thanks, my amazing tech-support guy.

Thank you, Mom, your interest and optimism means a lot to me. And for passing down the gift of music, I am forever blessed, grateful to you and Dad.

Thank you to my friend, Celia Buckles, for invaluable artistic and editing suggestions. I appreciate our coffee klatches, sharing ideas and laughs.

Heartfelt thanks to all my family members and friends who listened tirelessly, supplying feedback for fine-tuning the project. You are what making a difference looks like; I am nothing without you.

Very grateful to Chris Obert, of Pear Tree Publishing, for your professional advice and assistance in publishing my first children's book. Thank you for making the journey and end-result truly amazing.

And to my delightful young violin students who read the drafts, your laughter gave me wings to fly to the finish.

Things to look for in the story.

- What musical instrument does Davy play?

- How many pages have bunnies on them?

- What are the kids doing in the snow?

- What does Davy's sled turn into?

- How many little songs does Davy sing?

Things to think about.

Davy likes music. He is learning to play the violin and he likes to sing songs. Do you play a musical instrument? Do you like to sing?

Davy's friends like to make snowmen, have snowball fights, go skating and make snow angels. What do you like to do in the snow?

Davy has a fun imagination. He pretends that his sled turns into an airplane and that all of his clothes fly off. What do you imagine when you are sliding down a snow covered hill?